For Phoenix

Always one of us
Always a Lentner

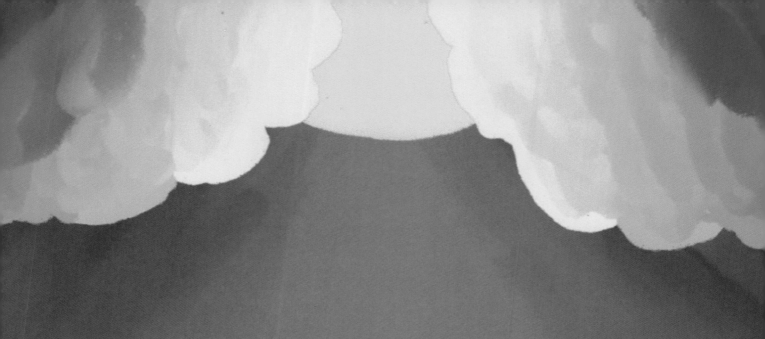

When the rain clouds parted
and drifted away,

Norman emerged to examine
the day.

The Sun was now proud and bright in the sky,

and Norman was hoping his washing would dry.

He hung up his clothes, one by one, on a line,

including his knickers, they
were one of a kind.

And when he had finished he went back inside,

happy as Larry and brimming with pride.

But who is this Larry?
Because something went
wrong;

he looked in his garden...
his knickers were gone!

Detective Papaya thought this crime was quite queer;

"it's the 15th time pants have been stolen this year".

There were no clues found at any crime scene,

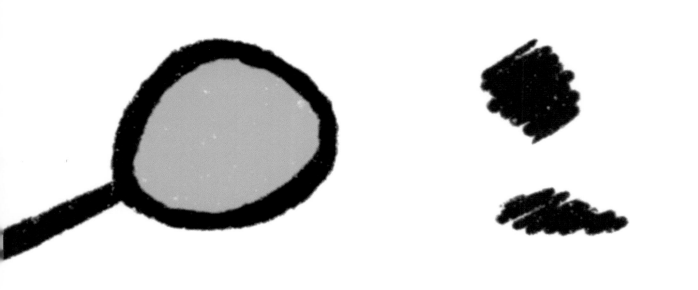

so Papaya devised the most devilish scheme.

He purchased a pair of fabulous knickers;

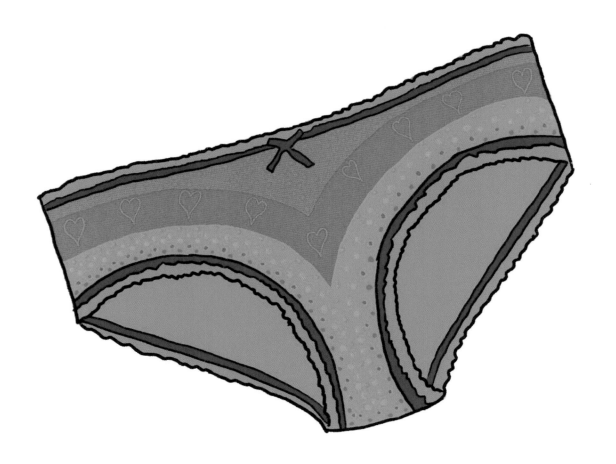

when the light shined upon them they danced and they flickered.

And then hid a bug that was very compact;

this bug would allow the pants to be tracked.

He hung them up high as the most tempting bait,

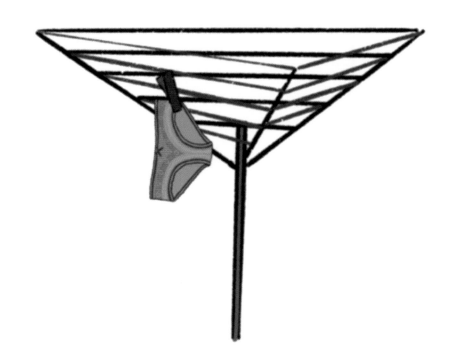

now all he could do was leave them and wait.

Constable Chickpea was tasked to keep watch,

a job that this copper could surely not botch.

He soon became tired, his eyes started to blink,

so he thought he would give them a couple of winks.

But when he awoke he was filled with pure dread,

the knickers were missing and his face turned bright red.

When Papaya found out he was not
at all pleased,

but he still had the bug so his mind
was at ease.

He used the bug to track the pants down,

they had stopped near a bank on the west side of town.

He made his way there as quick as can be,

to see mask wearing robbers beginning to flee.

He kicked down the door with his heavy right boot,

to find the two villains, bang to rights, with the loot.

They were using the knickers to
conceal their faces,

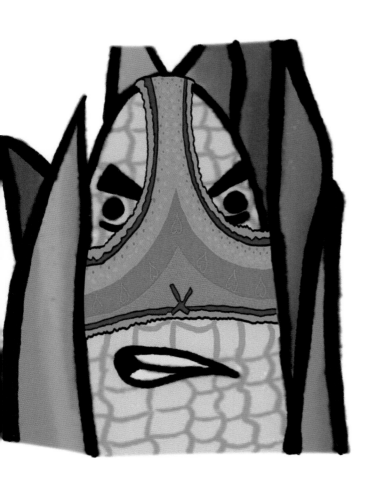

while they robbed banks and jewellers
and other such places.

There was Contemptible Corn who was villainous scum;

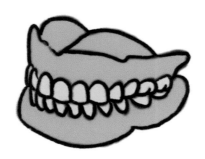

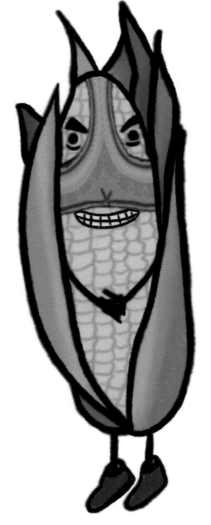

he once nicked false teeth from the mouth of his mum.

And Rancid Radish, a terrible beast;

the shops had no bread as he'd stolen the yeast.

Detective Papaya read their rights straight away,

and justice had once again had its day.

They were found guilty at court and banged up for good measure,

to spend twenty years at her Majesty's pleasure.

Norman rejoiced, "he's my hero, my messiah",

"not at all" he replied,
"I'm just Detective Papaya".

Printed in Great Britain
by Amazon